Beech Farm

Walter's Garage

Mallard Pond

Wildwood Brook

For Kerrie—C.R.

Library of Congress Cataloging in Publication Data
Laird, Elizabeth. The day Sidney ran off / by Elizabeth Laird ;
pictures by Colin Reeder. p.   cm.—(A little red tractor book)
Summary: Duncan the tractor helps Stan
the farmer look for a missing piglet.
ISBN 0-688-10241-7 (trade)—ISBN 0-688-10242-5 (lib.)
[1. Tractors—Fiction. 2. Pigs—Fiction. 3. Farms—Fiction.]
I. Reeder, Colin, ill. II. Title. III. Series.
PZ7.L1579Day 1991 [E]—dc20 90-11154 CIP AC
Printed in Portugal
First U.S. edition 1991
1 3 5 7 9 10 8 6 4 2

A Little Red Tractor Book

The Day Sidney
Ran Off

ELIZABETH LAIRD

pictures by COLIN REEDER

TAMBOURINE BOOKS · NEW YORK

It was hot in the yard at Gosling Farm. The swallows darted in and out of the barn with food for their babies. The sun sparkled on the bright paint of Duncan, the little red tractor. Stan the farmer looked up at the clear blue sky. "Before we go make hay," he said "we'll have to water the pigs." He hitched up the trailer to Duncan. Then he lifted the water tank onto the trailer and filled it up with clean water. "All ready," said Stan. "Off we go."

The piglets were glad to see Duncan and raced up to him. They squealed and pushed and squirmed round his front wheels. They couldn't wait to slurp and snuffle in the nice ice-cold water. Stan looked at the piglets. "Seven, eight, nine—" he counted. "Wait a minute. Where's Sidney?"

Stan looked around the mother pig. He looked behind the trough. He looked under Duncan and in the pigs' shed and over the hedge. The piglet wasn't there. "Sidney's got out of the field again," said Stan, scratching his head. "Hanged if I know how he does it. We'll have to go and find him."

Stan drove Duncan back to the farmyard. "Come on," he said. "Get a move on." He was in a hurry to find Sidney. But Duncan couldn't go any faster. "Bit sluggish this morning," said Stan. "What's the matter with you?" He backed Duncan up to the barn and unhooked the trailer. Then he looked about for Sidney. The hens didn't like Stan poking about in their favorite dark corners. They squawked and flapped and pecked crossly. "All right, don't fuss," said Stan. "I'm only looking for Sidney."

Stan drove Duncan into Five Oaks Pasture. The cows were resting under the trees in the shade, flicking at the flies with their tufty tails. It was all quiet and peaceful. There was no sign of Sidney here. "Sidney!" called Stan, just to make sure. But Sidney wasn't there. Duncan chugged slowly over to the gate again. "Maybe you need an oil change," said Stan.

Duncan turned out of the field, and Stan gave a shout. There was Sidney trotting down the road in front of them. "Little scamp," said Stan. "Bet he wants to get down to the river. He'll wriggle under the gate into the sheep field."

Duncan set off after Sidney, but his engine started to cough. "I know what's wrong with you," said Stan. "Spot of dirt in your fuel pipe." He revved Duncan's engine up hard. Whoosh! That was better. Duncan was ready for action now. Stan leaned out of Duncan's cab and looked down the road. It was just as he'd thought. Sidney was squeezing under the gate, heading for the river.

Duncan raced down the road and turned into the sheep field. "There he is!" shouted Stan. "Come on now, Duncan! We'll catch him down by the willow!" Sidney ran straight across the field and into the water. It splashed around his trotters and dripped off his tail. He bent his head for a long, cool drink. Then suddenly Sidney saw the ducks. He splashed after them. The ducks quacked and flapped and flew off into the wood. Sidney looked around for something else to chase.

Duncan and Stan stopped on the river bank. "Come on, Sidney," called Stan. "Time to go home." Sidney took no notice. A minnow swam past his leg. Sidney put his head down to look and got a noseful of water. "Ah-choo!" Sidney sneezed, lost his balance, and rolled over into the water with a splash. He stood up, and rolled over again. This was fun! "Come on, will you!" shouted Stan. But Sidney still took no notice.

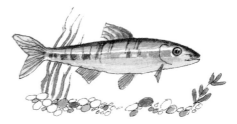

Stan shook his head, and patted Duncan's hood. "We'll have to use a bit of cunning," he said. He put his hand in his pocket and pulled out a carrot. Sidney put his head to one side and looked at it. He liked carrots. Stan put the carrot on the ground. He hid behind Duncan's rear wheel and waited. Sidney lifted his wet shiny snout and sniffed. He couldn't see Stan, but he could see the carrot, all juicy and crunchy and sweet. Sidney took one step toward the bank, and then he took another. Stan peeped out from behind the tractor. "Here he comes now, Duncan," he whispered.

Sidney dashed forward, grabbed the carrot, and started to run back into the water. Stan jumped up, arms outstretched. Sidney squealed. Stan leaped forward and fell with a squelch into the mud. "Oh! You little devil!" shouted Stan, but he had caught Sidney, carrot and all.

Stan stood up. He was covered in mud, and so was the piglet he held in his arms. Sidney wriggled happily. He liked the mud. Stan climbed back into Duncan's cab and Sidney put his muddy snout out the window. Duncan bumped over the rough grass. His engine was going fine now. He was firing on all cylinders, and ready for the haymaking.

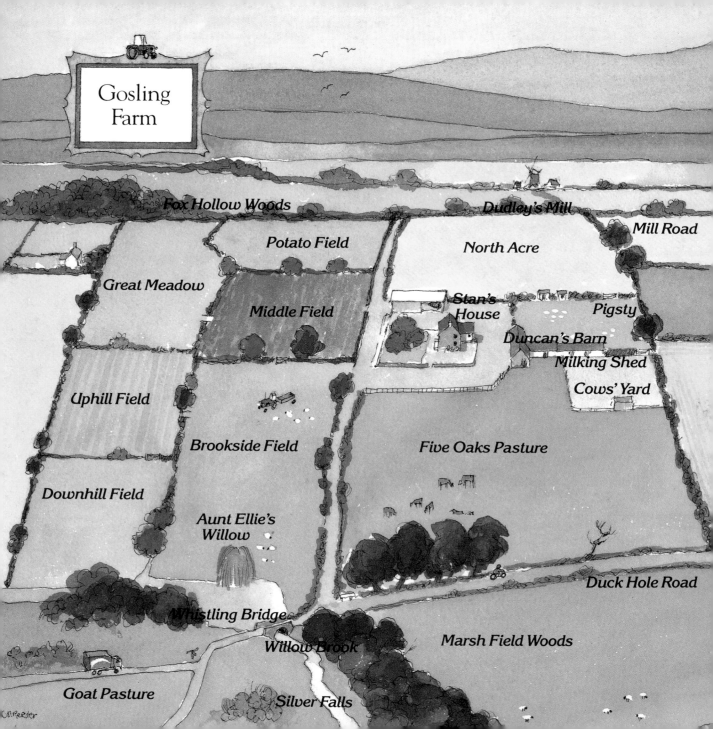

Gosling Farm

Fox Hollow Woods

Dudley's Mill

Mill Road

Potato Field

North Acre

Great Meadow

Middle Field

Stan's House

Pigsty

Duncan's Barn

Milking Shed

Cows' Yard

Uphill Field

Brookside Field

Five Oaks Pasture

Downhill Field

Aunt Ellie's Willow

Duck Hole Road

Whistling Bridge

Willow Brook

Marsh Field Woods

Goat Pasture

Silver Falls